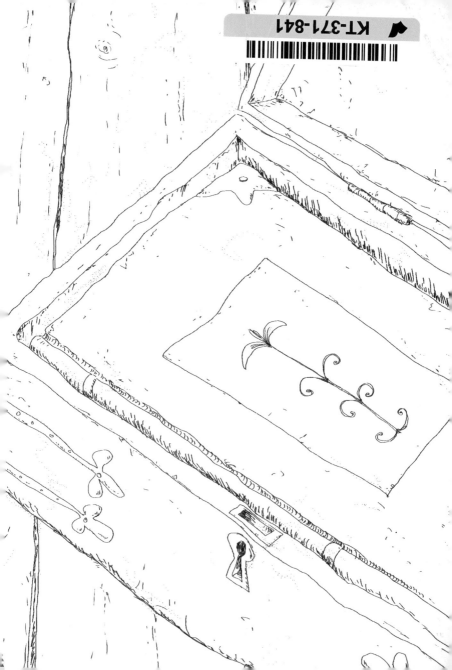

JOE O'BRIEN is an award-winning gardener who lives in Ballyfermot in Dublin. This is his ninth book about the wonderful world of Alfie Green. He has also written two books in the 'Danny Wilde' series for older readers: *Little Croker* and *Féile Fever*.

DEDICATION
The *Alfie Green* series is dedicated to my son, Ethan, who in his short time in this world taught me to be strong, happy and thankful for the gift of life. Thank you, Ethan, for the inspiration to write.

Alfie Green and the Chocolate Cosmos is dedicated to Megan, Dylan, Ross and Alex.

ACKNOWLEDGEMENTS:
A big thank you to all at The O'Brien Press, to Jean Texier, and, of course, to my readers.

*　　　　*　　　　*

JEAN TEXIER is a storyboard artist and illustrator. Initially trained in animation, he has worked in the film industry for many years.

ALFIE GREEN AND THE CHOCOLATE COSMOS

Joe O'Brien

Illustrated by Jean Texier

THE O'BRIEN PRESS
DUBLIN

First published 2010 by The O'Brien Press Ltd.,
12 Terenure Road East, Rathgar, Dublin 6, Ireland.
Tel: +353 1 4923333; Fax: +353 1 4922777
E-mail: books@obrien.ie
Website: www.obrien.ie

ISBN: 978-1-84717-196-2

British Library Cataloguing-in-Publication Data
A catalogue record for this title is available from the British Library

1 2 3 4 5 6 7 8 9 10
10 11 12 13 14 15

The O'Brien Press receives
assistance from

Editing, typesetting, layout, design: The O'Brien Press Ltd.
Illustrations: Jean Texier
Printed and bound by Scandbook AB, Sweden.
The paper in this book is produced using pulp from managed forests.

CONTENTS

CHAPTER 1

THEY'RE LATE

'Alfie! Stop looking out of the window,' said Mrs Green crossly. 'Sit down and finish your breakfast. It's almost time for school.'

'But where are the trucks, Mam?' Alfie asked. 'Why hasn't the chocolate arrived?'

Every year Budsville held a special fair in memory of Harry 'Chockie' Chaplin who was born on Budsville Avenue.

Harry's chocolate factory was the most famous in the world, and every year two HUGE trucks would arrive with boxes and boxes of chocolates for the fair.

The chocolates came in different shapes for every fair; last year's were animal-shaped.

It was Alfie's job to arrange the chocolates on the stalls set up on the green beside his house.

'They're late,' said Alfie.

'Don't worry, Alfie,' said his mother. 'I'm sure the chocolate will be here when you get home from school.'

But when Alfie and his pal Fitzer raced back from school there were no trucks. And there were no boxes of chocolates.

Lucy was standing at the front door, with a piece of paper in her hand.

'This came for you,' said Lucy as she handed it to Alfie.

Alfie noticed that the edges of the paper were nibbled and damp.

'Mammy says it's really bad news. So I tried to get Posh and Becks to eat it!' Lucy explained.

'Oh no!' Alfie gasped as he read the note. 'This is awful.'

'What does it say?' Fitzer asked anxiously.

'The chocolate fair is cancelled,' Alfie said sadly. 'There was a flood at Mr Chaplin's factory and all the chocolates for the fair were ruined.'

Fitzer's face fell. 'I was really looking forward to it,' he said. 'I LOVE Chockie's chocolates, especially the white chocolate polar bears from last year. They were my favourite.'

Just then, Mrs Butler from next door appeared.

'This came through the letterbox,' she said. 'Is it true, Alfie? Will there be no fair this year?'

'I'm afraid so, Mrs Butler.'

Poor Mrs Butler! Her face got very old and wrinkly all of a sudden, and a small tear ran down her cheek.

13

Now she would have no Chockie's chocolates to make her famous chocolate cake and the special sauce for her strawberry ice-cream.

As she walked back to her house, Alfie could see her sniffing into her handkerchief.

It's not FAIR, he thought. Then he made up his mind.

'I'm going to do something about it!' he said out loud.

'But what can you do?' asked Fitzer.

'I don't know yet,' Alfie said, 'but just you wait and see.'

CHAPTER 2

A CHOCOLATE MOON

When Fitzer had gone, Alfie went out to the garden shed. He lifted the loose floorboard and took the magical book out of its box.

He put his hand on the first page.

The wise old plant rose up, stretching its leaves and straightening its glasses.

'Hello Alfie,' said the wise old plant. 'Got another problem for me?'

'Yes,' Alfie replied, 'a BIG problem.'

'Did you ever hear of the Budsville chocolate fair?' he asked.

'Indeed I did,' said the plant. 'Your grandfather often talked about it.'

'Well,' said Alfie, 'it's cancelled. Not happening. No fair this year.'

'Oh, we can't have that,' said the wise old plant. 'Let's see if there is anything in the book that can help.'

He began to flick over the pages of the magical book.

'There!' he said, pointing, 'I knew it was here somewhere.'

As Alfie was about to look in the book something dark and soft rolled down the page. He caught it just before it hit the floor.

'It's CHOCOLATE!' he exclaimed, sucking his finger.

'Yes,' said the wise old plant. 'It comes from the Chocolate Cosmos.'

'Wow!'

Alfie looked at the pages and couldn't believe his eyes. It was like looking into space – except that everything was made of chocolate. There were dark chocolate asteroids, gleaming white chocolate stars and a pale chocolate moon.

'How can a cosmos be made of chocolate?' Alfie asked.

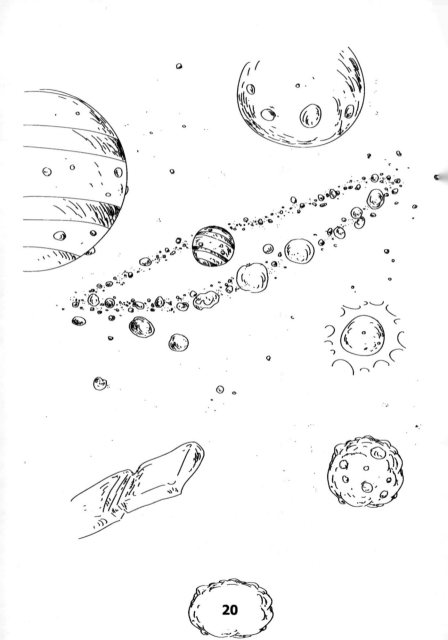

'That's where chocolate came from,' said the wise old plant.

'From **outer space**?' asked Alfie.

'Yes,' insisted the wise old plant. 'Maybe not in your world, but certainly in my world.'

He told Alfie how, many many years ago, a chocolate-filled comet had **THUNDERED** through the sky above Arcania and crashed deep into the Roaring Rainforest.

Chocolate seeds scattered on the forest bed and almost overnight a new type of plant grew from the seeds.

These weren't like any of the other plants in Arcania. They didn't talk. They didn't have magical powers. They were sweet-smelling, delicious **chocolate** plants.

CHAPTER 3

A WARNING

'So,' said the wise old plant, 'maybe you *could* have your chocolate fair this year after all. Of course, you would have to go to the Roaring Rainforest for some chocolate seeds.'

'No problem!' said Alfie.

The wise old plant shook his head.

'Not so fast, Alfie,' he warned. 'The Roaring Rainforest is full of dangers. Especially the chocolate vine that twines around the strangled tree.'

'What's so scary about a chocolate vine?' Alfie asked.

'The end of that vine is the gateway to the Chocolate Cosmos. If you cross the gateway you will never return to Earth. Not even your crystal

orchid will be able to help you.'

Alfie looked worried. That didn't sound good at all. Then he thought of Mrs Butler and all the others who would be so disappointed if the fair didn't happen.

'I'll do it,' he said firmly.

'Well, if you're sure, here is what you must do,' said the wise old plant. 'Go deep into the Roaring Rainforest until you smell chocolate. Search under the chocolate plants and you will find the seeds you need for your fair.'

With a final warning about the chocolate vine, the wise old plant folded itself back into the book, which closed with a

CHAPTER 4

ARCANIA AGAIN

Alfie stood outside the shed, with the Crystal Orchid in his pocket.

'Paddy! Jimmy! Vinny! Mick!' he called out to his tool friends. 'Is anyone here?'

There was a rustling noise from some bushes up ahead.

Out hopped Vinny the fork, followed by Paddy the spade and Mick the hoe.

'Hello lads,' Alfie greeted them.
'Good to see you.'

He looked around for Jimmy the clippers.

'Isn't Jimmy with you?'

'No,' said Paddy, 'he's chasing some terrible teasing thistles.'

'What brings you to Arcania?' asked Mick.

Alfie told them about the chocolate fair and why he needed to get to the Roaring Rainforest.

'The Roaring Rainforest? I was there once,' said Vinny. 'It gave me a bad case of rust.'

'But you can show me where it is?' Alfie asked excitedly.

'Oh yes,' Vinny replied. 'I just wouldn't want to go in.'

'Do you see those dark clouds?' Paddy pointed to the skies over the far east of Arcania.

Alfie nodded.

'Those are the everlasting clouds that cover the Roaring Rainforest. That's the way we must go.'

They had walked a long way when Alfie noticed that Paddy kept looking behind him.

'What's the matter, Paddy?' he asked.

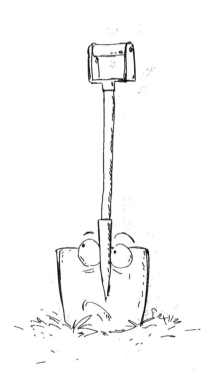

'I think we're being **followed**,' Paddy whispered. 'Listen!'

They all stopped. There was a strange, scratchy, creeping sound.

Suddenly, out from behind some trees came a platoon of spider plants.

'It's an attack!' yelled Vinny. 'Run, Alfie, run! We'll fight them off!'

'And don't look back!' added Mick.

Alfie ran as fast as his legs could carry him.

He did look back, just once. He saw Paddy and Mick batting the spiders to Vinny, who caught them on his prongs and flicked them high into the sky.

CHAPTER 5

THE ROARING RAINFOREST

Glad that his friends were okay, Alfie ran faster and faster towards the clouded sky.

CRASH!

A trip web spun by the spider plants brought Alfie to the ground, head first.

He was knocked out.

Alfie woke to the sound of whispering. It grew louder and louder and **louder** until his head was filled with a roaring noise. He must be in the Roaring Rainforest!

He opened his eyes and discovered that he couldn't move his arms or his legs. He was trapped in a web cocoon made by the spider plants that had carried him to the Rainforest.

The roaring went on... and on... and on. Finally Alfie understood what it was saying:

'WHO DARES TO ROAM THE ROARING RAINFOREST?'

Alfie leaned his head back as far as he could, took a deep breath, then bravely roared back:

'ALFIE GREENnnnnnn! I've come to collect **SEEDS** from the **CHOCOLATE PLANTS.'**

There was silence, then a fearsome bellow from the forest.

'The seeds belong to ME! Anyone

who tried to take them must face the **Forest Ogre.'**

Ogre? Alfie wasn't sure what an ogre was, but it didn't sound good.

THUMP! The ground beneath Alfie's feet shook and cracked. All the spider plants ran for cover.

THUMP! THUMP! THUMP!

CHAPTER 6

WHAT'S AN OGRE?

A large green creature stomped slowly towards Alfie. Small, evil black eyes were sunk into its huge bald head. Its great hole of a mouth was drooling.

'Yuck!' Alfie had never seen anything as horrible. He struggled to free his arms. If only he could reach the Crystal Orchid in his pocket!

The Ogre drew closer and closer. Its gigantic fists reached out for Alfie.

43

Alfie had almost given up hope when he heard: 'Alfieee!'

It was Jimmy the clippers. He had sorted out the terrible teasing thistles and was on his way home when he spotted Alfie being carried off by the spider plants.

'Hurry, Jimmy!' Alfie shouted. 'I can't get free.'

Jimmy bladed over to Alfie's side.

SNIP! SNIP! SNIP!

'Nice one!' cheered Alfie as Jimmy snipped the last piece of sticky web that held Alfie captive.

The web sprang open and Alfie jumped out, just as the Ogre charged – and ran straight into the sticky prison!

'Uff! Aargh! ' the Ogre growled as it tried to pull the web from its face.

Alfie and Jimmy sped away from the danger, like two racing cars heading for the winning line.

But the Roaring Rainforest wasn't finished with Alfie yet!

45

It bellowed up at the everlasting
clouds: **'They're getting away,
now rain save the day!'**

46

CHAPTER 7

SWEPT AWAY

Raindrops as big as garden ponds fell from the clouds. The ground beneath Alfie's feet turned to mud.

'**LANDSLIDE!**' yelled Jimmy, and he used his pointy blades to climb up a tree to safety.

Alfie tried to follow him but a huge wave of muddy water knocked him over and he was swept along the forest floor. Behind him came the army of spider plants and the Forest Ogre.

Suddenly Alfie felt something grab his foot and he was swung up into the air. He had been plucked out of danger by a Trapeze Vine.

'Yahoooo!' cheered Alfie as he was swung upside down from one vine to another, high over the rushing water.

'Good luck, Alfie!' called Jimmy. 'Be careful that your Crystal Orchid doesn't fall out of your pocket.'

'Don't worry, Jimmy, the Crystal Orchid can only come out by the hand of the keeper,' Alfie shouted back. 'IT CAN'T FALL Ouuuuut!'

And he disappeared
deeper into the forest.

CHAPTER 8

FOUND THEM!

Alfie began to feel sick. He wasn't used to being upside down for so long. And the air was filled with a sweet, sticky smell, almost like hot chocolate.

CHOCOLATE???

He sniffed. Yes! He'd made it to the chocolate plants.

'Can I get down, please?' he asked.

The Trapeze Vine gently lowered Alfie to the ground. His head was dizzy and his legs were a bit wobbly from flying through the air.

The forest floor was covered in the most unusual plants Alfie had ever seen – and they were all made of **chocolate**. There were planets, stars, moons, even comets.

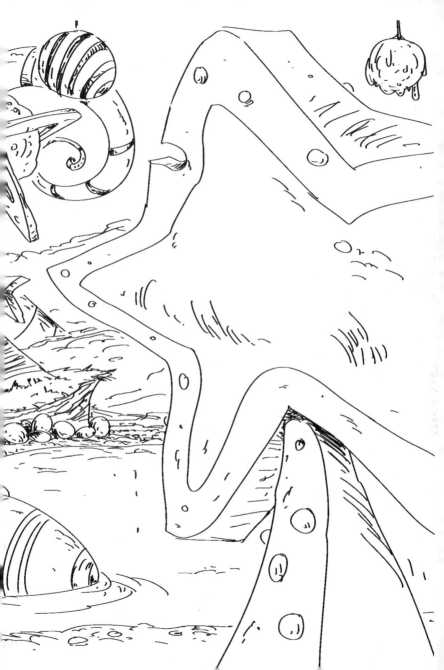

Alfie got on his knees and began to collect the seeds. He didn't stop until his pockets – except the one with the Crystal Orchid – were ready to burst.

That's my work done, thought Alfie. Time to go home.

Just then he spotted a plant that was completely different to all the others.

It had HUGE leaves and twisting stems that wound around a dead tree – up and up until you couldn't see the top of the plant.

I must get some of those seeds, he
thought. He could just picture the
plant winding all the way round the
green and over his garden wall.

Poor Alfie! He'd forgotten the wise old plant's warning about the chocolate vine that twined around the strangled tree.

As he leaned over to pick up some seeds, four chocolate tendrils curled around his wrists and ankles. He was *CATAPULTED* up into the air like a bungee jump going backwards.

Alfie was rocketed through the air at COSMIC speed. Soon he was way past the clouds over the Roaring Rainforest.

59

When he looked up he could see the end of the chocolate vine.

Oh no! Alfie needed to get hold of his Crystal Orchid – FAST!

He began to bite into the chocolate that was wrapped around his wrist. He chomped and chomped until his whole face was covered with chocolate. At last there was a SNAP, and suddenly he was FREE.

He reached into his pocket for the Crystal Orchid.

BUT WAS IT TOO LATE?

Just as the Chocolate Vine shot
Alfie towards the gateway to the
Chocolate Cosmos, there was a flash
of blinding light!

ALFIE HAD MADE IT! He was
home.

Alfie hugged his Crystal Orchid and whispered 'thank you' before he put it back in its biscuit tin.

He locked the shed door after him and ran into the house.

CHAPTER 9

THE BEST EVER

Lucy was quick to notice Alfie's chocolate-covered face.

'Daddy!' she screamed. 'Alfie's had chocolate and he didn't share any with me.'

'Shush, Lucy!' said Alfie, 'Tomorrow you can have all the chocolate you ever dreamed of.'

'Really? You promise?'

'I promise!'

Then he ran upstairs and emptied all the seeds into a paper bag.

That night, Alfie sneaked out of the house with his bag of chocolate seeds. He scattered them all over the green until there wasn't a single seed left.

'Now, GROW!' he said, as loudly as he could without waking any of the neighbours.

It felt like he had only just closed his eyes when Lucy came rushing into his room, screaming her head off.

'Alfie, wake up! The chocolate I dreamed of last night is here.'

Alfie rubbed the sleep from his eyes and then jumped out of bed.

He threw his clothes on quicker than you can say 'too much chocolate will make you sick' and bolted out of the house.

The WHOLE of Budsville Avenue seemed to be on the green: Mrs Butler, Mr Skully, Old Podge Kelly, Mad Aggie, Fitzer and his mam and dad, Alfie's granny. Even Whacker Walsh was there, stuffing his face from the hundreds of chocolate plants that covered the grass. It was a real chocolate FEAST.

'THEY GREW!' whooped Alfie, running over to his pal.

'What grew, Alfie?' asked Fitzer.

Before he could think of an answer, Mrs Butler came running over.

'Oh, Alfie,' she said, 'isn't it wonderful! The people in the factory must have worked all night to make new chocolates for our fair.'

'Yes,' said Fitzer, 'and what a great idea: Plants from the Chocolate Cosmos.'

What! thought Alfie. How did Fitzer know that?

Then he saw the sign:

Welcome to Budsville Chocolate Fair

Featuring

PLANTS FROM THE
CHOCOLATE COSMOS.

Enjoy!

Chaplin's Chocks

Alfie was confused. Where had *that* come from?

Then, just for a second, a tiny blue sparkle shimmered around the sign.

71

Alfie watched as it rose up and
drifted across the green, over his wall,
and disappeared into the garden shed.

Only Alfie had noticed the sparkle. And only Alfie – and the wise old plant – knew that these really were: PLANTS FROM THE CHOCOLATE COSMOS!

READ ALFIE'S OTHER GREAT

ADVENTURES IN:

PRAISE FOR THE

ALFIE GREEN SERIES

'Gorgeous books, beautifully illustrated.'
Sunday Independent

'A great choice for boys and girls.'
Irish Independent

'Bright, breezy and full of flesh crawling incidents.
Young readers will love this.'
Village

'... engaging, action-packed story. Beautifully produced.'
Inis Magazine

'Best writer ever.' Siobhan Quigley (age 8)
Laois Voice

'*Alfie Green and the Magical Gift* was the best book
I have ever read in my life.' Hannah Meaney (age 7)
Clare People

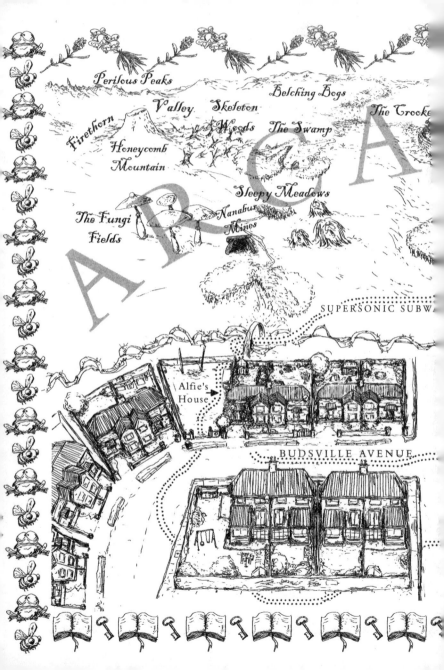